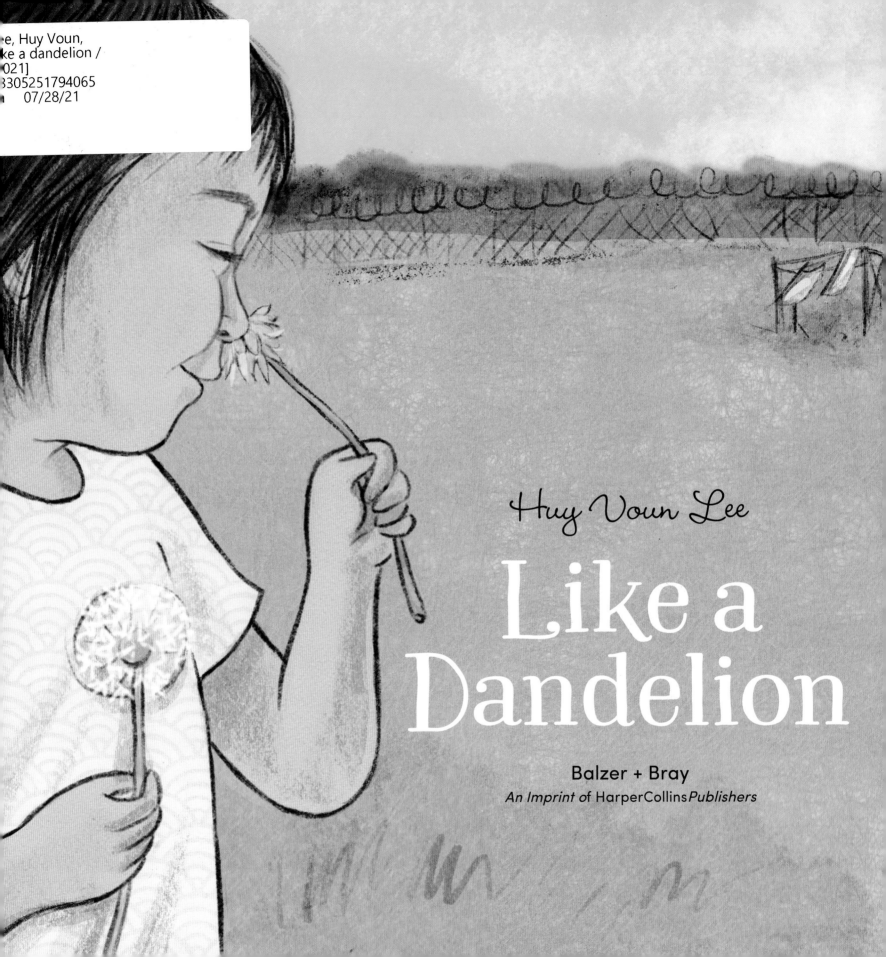

Huy Voun Lee

Like a Dandelion

Balzer + Bray
An Imprint of HarperCollins*Publishers*

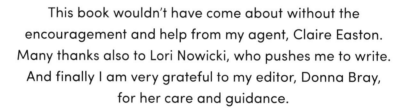

This book wouldn't have come about without the
encouragement and help from my agent, Claire Easton.
Many thanks also to Lori Nowicki, who pushes me to write.
And finally I am very grateful to my editor, Donna Bray,
for her care and guidance.

Balzer + Bray is an imprint of HarperCollins Publishers.

Like a Dandelion
Copyright © 2021 by Huy Voun Lee
All rights reserved. Manufactured in Italy.

ISBN 978-0-06-299373-1

The artist used Procreate and Photoshop to create the digital illustrations for this book.
Typography by Dana Fritts
21 22 23 24 25 RTLO 10 9 8 7 6 5 4 3 2 1
❖
First Edition

I dedicate this book to my parents and siblings, with whom I shared this journey; to the immigrants who came before us; and to the American people who opened their hearts in welcoming us. They are the people who truly make America beautiful.

Like feathery seeds,
we take flight,

finding a new home

even
in
the
tiniest
space.

We put down roots
in unfamiliar soil

and nourish ourselves
through the winter slumber.

Like a dandelion,
at first I am shy.

But I raise my face to the sun

and the rain.

In springtime, clouds blow over
and buds blossom.

We make golden garlands
in a field of a hundred suns.

Bees come for the nectar,
bunnies come for the flowers.

In autumn, winds whisk in,
scattering new seeds around us.

Like a dandelion, I am strong and giving,
planted happily in soil that I now call home.

Author's Note

Dandelions are flowering plants indigenous to Eurasia. They have been cultivated for food and as an herb since ancient times, and the Chinese have used them for medicine for over a thousand years. Some people think dandelions were brought over to North America on the *Mayflower* for their health benefits. Now many people consider them pesky weeds that invade their lawns, although others have rediscovered the usefulness of the dandelion.

The author (second from left) at age five with her brother, Chin-shing (far left); two unknown girls; and her sister, Mong-Sing, at a Cambodian refugee camp in Utapao, Thailand, before their eventual immigration to the United States in 1975.

Photo courtesy of the author